The Gunniwolf

RETOLD BY

Wilhelmina Harper

ILLUSTRATED BY

Barbara Upton

DUTTON CHILDREN'S BOOKS
NEW YORK

For my sisters, Pam and Martha,
and the little girls we were together
B.U.

Original copyright © 1918 by Wilhelmina Harper
Text copyright © 2003 by Dutton Children's Books
Illustrations copyright © 2003 by Barbara Upton
All rights reserved.

CIP Data is available.

Published in the United States 2003
by Dutton Children's Books,
a division of Penguin Putnam Books for Young Readers
345 Hudson Street, New York, New York 10014
www.penguinputnam.com

Designed by Irene Vandervoort
Manufactured in China
First Edition
ISBN 0-525-46785-8
1 2 3 4 5 6 7 8 9 10

ABOUT THE STORY

The Gunniwolf is an American folktale whose origin is uncertain. Tales like this one come out of the oral tradition, the passing down of narrative and folklore from one generation of storytellers to another. And since the tales weren't written, they changed with the teller, thus allowing them to take on different forms. They spread as people traveled, and then changed some more, becoming part of what Lloyd Alexander has called the "cauldron of story." They belonged to no one—and to everyone. And that is why so many variants of some of our most well-known stories exist, representing diverse regions of the world.

These stories were meant to entertain, of course, but they served other purposes as well: to scare, to instruct, to ridicule, to explain, and to warn, among others. The story of the gunniwolf is what is known as a cautionary tale. The purpose of this kind of tale was to serve as a warning to the children of a village or settlement not to wander too far from home, not to stray into the surrounding woods or, as in this case, the jungle.

This story may remind readers of the more familiar *Little Red Riding Hood*, or *Little Red Cap*, as it is known in the Brothers Grimm version. Also a cautionary tale, that story was originally collected by Jacob and Wilhelm Grimm, who in the early nineteenth century traveled all over Germany, listening to and recording stories the people told. *Little Red Cap* and *The Gunniwolf* both feature a little girl, a wolf, and a mother who cautions the child. But *Little Red Cap* is a much harsher tale. The wolf eats the grandmother whom the little girl sets out to visit, and after deceiving the child so as to eat her too, he is killed by hunters, who rescue her and then cut open his stomach to free the grandmother.

In *The Gunniwolf,* nobody dies. We are not ever really sure of the wolf's intentions toward the little girl. The wolf asks Little Girl only to sing to him, and thus the story is related to a different folktale motif: By singing a song, a captive gradually moves away and then escapes.

In the version of the story collected by Wilhelmina Harper, the expression *guten, sweeten* is certainly reminiscent of the German; the "jungle" reference seems to imply African overtones. (In this book, the jungle has been transmuted into an American rural setting.) Including *The Gunniwolf* in *Twenty Tellable Tales,* Margaret Read MacDonald notes:

> There is an Eskimo variant . . . in which mouse tricks fox, and another variant from
> the Russian steppes in which sheep escape from a wolf. Stith Thompson lists Kaffir and
> Cape Verde Island variants of this motif.

The origin of the actual term *gunniwolf* (sometimes spelled *gunny wolf*) remains unknown as well, but it might refer to the brownish color of a gunny, or burlap, sack. Or it might be related to the term *cunning*. In some of the stories that African slaves brought to America, there is a "cunning" animal, such as a fox or a hare, who gets the better of a bigger animal or predator.

The real appeal of this story, which has made it a classic irrespective of its origins, is that it begs to be read aloud. With its cadences, onomatopoeic words, and dialect songs, it should be passed on to a new generation, just as storytellers did hundreds of years ago.

There was once a little girl who lived with her mother very close to a dense jungle. Each day the mother would caution Little Girl to be most careful and never enter the jungle, because—if she did—the Gunniwolf might get her! Little Girl always promised that she would never, NEVER even go NEAR the jungle.

One day the mother had to go away for a while. Her last words were to caution Little Girl that whatever else she did, she must keep far away from the jungle!

And Little Girl was very sure that she would not go anywhere *near* it.

The mother was hardly out of sight, however, when Little Girl noticed some beautiful white flowers growing at the very edge of the jungle.

"Oh," she thought, "wouldn't I love to have some of those—I'll pick just a few."

Then, forgetting all about the warning, she began to gather the white flowers, all the while singing happily to herself: *"Kum-kwa, khi-wa, kum-kwa, khi-wa."*

All of a sudden she noticed, a little farther in the jungle,

some beautiful *pink* flowers growing. "Oh," she thought,
"I must surely gather some of those, too!"

On she tripped, farther into the jungle, and began
picking the pink flowers, all the while singing happily:
"Kum-kwa, khi-wa, kum-kwa, khi-wa."

When she had her arms full of white and pink flowers,
she peeped a little farther . . .

and way in the middle of the jungle she saw some
beautiful *orange* flowers growing.

"Oh," she thought, "I'll take just a few of those, and what a pretty bouquet I'll have to show my mother!"

So she gathered the orange flowers, too, singing to herself all the while: *"Kum-kwa, khi-wa, kum-kwa, khi-wa,"* when SUDDENLY—

UP ROSE THE GUNNIWOLF!

He said, "Little Girl, why for you move?"

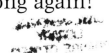

Tremblingly she answered, "I no move."

The Gunniwolf said, "Then you sing that guten, sweeten song again!"

So she sang: *"Kum-kwa, khi-wa, kum-kwa, khi-wa,"*
and then—

the old Gunniwolf nodded his head and fell fast asleep.

Away ran Little Girl as fast as ever she could—
PIT-pat, PIT-pat, PIT-pat, PIT-pat, PIT-pat.

Then the Gunniwolf woke up!

Away he ran—hunker-CHA, hunker-CHA, hunker-CHA...

until he caught up to her. And he said, "Little Girl, why for you move?"

"I no move," she answered.

"Then you sing that guten, sweeten song again!"

Timidly she sang: *"Kum-kwa, khi-wa, kum-kwa, khi-wa."*
Then the old Gunniwolf nodded, nodded, and went
sound asleep.

Away ran Little Girl just as fast as ever she could—
PIT-pat, PIT-pat, PIT-pat, PIT-pat, PIT-pat—
and again the Gunniwolf woke up! Away he ran—
hunker-CHA, hunker-CHA, hunker-CHA, hunker-CHA—
PIT-pat, PIT-pat, PIT-pat—

hunker-CHA, hunker-CHA—

until he caught up to her and said, "Little Girl, why for you move?"

"I no move."

"Then you sing that guten, sweeten song again!"

So she sang: *"Kum-kwa, khi-wa, kum-kwa, khi-wa,"* until
the old Gunniwolf again nodded, nodded, and fell asleep.

Then AWAY ran Little Girl—

PIT-pat, PIT-pat, PIT-pat, PIT-pat—

until she came almost to the edge of the jungle!

PIT-pat, PIT-pat, PIT-pat, PIT-pat—

until she got away out of the jungle!

PIT-pat, PITTY-pat, PIT-pat, PITTY-pat—

until she reached her very own door.

From that day to this, Little Girl has never, NEVER gone into the jungle.